This Little Tiger book
belongs to:

_____

_____

_____

LITTLE TIGER PRESS
1 The Coda Centre,
189 Munster Road, London SW6 6AW
www.littletiger.co.uk

First published in Great Britain 2013
This edition published 2014
Text copyright © Julia Hubery 2013 • Illustrations copyright © Caroline Pedler 2013
Julia Hubery and Caroline Pedler have asserted their rights to be identified as the author
and illustrator of this work under the Copyright, Designs and Patents Act, 1988
A CIP catalogue record for this book is available from the British Library

ISBN 978-1-84895-654-4
LTP/1800/0763/0514
Printed in China
2 4 6 8 10 9 7 5 3 1

To Mark, James, Joe and Jess ~ JH

For all my friends, without them lots of great things would never have happened! ~ CP

That's What

Friends Are For

Julia Hubery · Caroline Pedler

LITTLE TIGER PRESS
London

"I love-love-love
my new jumper!" sang little
Alfie Bear, dancing round
the room.

"It's the **bestest** jumper **ever!**"

"I knitted it just for you," smiled
  Mummy, "so there's love
  in every stitch!"

"Wow, thank you!"
said Alfie.

"I must show Moley!
And Rabbit! And **everybody**!"
And off he raced.

"Moley, **Moley,
Mo-leeey**!"
called Alfie.

"Oh bother, nobody's home," he sighed.
But what was that eeky-squeaky noise
in the bushes?

It was
Moley!

"Help!" he squeaked.
"I was picking blackberries,
and I've got stuck in their
pesky prickles!"

"I'll help you out," said Alfie. And with a wriggle, a jiggle and a tug, Moley was safe and sound.

But Alfie's jumper
wasn't.

It was icky with blackberry blotches,
and the prickles had torn a hole.
"My **new** jumper!" cried Alfie.

"My mummy
made it for me!"

"Don't worry, Alfie," said Moley.
"We can wash it in the stream, come on."

As they hurried along, they heard a **huffing** and **puffing** in Rabbit's garden.

"Alfie! Help!" called Rabbit. "My daddy's grown the most **monster** carrot! But it just **won't** come up!"

"Let's all pull together," said Alfie.

"One…two…three…

HEAVE!!!"

POP!

went the carrot,
and . . .

SPLAT!

went the friends as
they plopped on their
bottoms in the mud.

"Alfie, you're a **mud monster!**" laughed Rabbit.
"Oh no!" said Moley. "That's Alfie's new jumper.
His mummy made it."
"With love in every
stitch!" sniffed Alfie.

"We must get you clean," said Rabbit,
and they rushed to the stream.

All together they rubbed and scrubbed, and squidged and squeezed.

Then they hung the soggy jumper up to dry in the sun.

"Oh!" said Alfie, when he put it on. "It's stretched!"

Moley nodded. "Maybe we'd better go home, before anything else happens to it."

But as the three friends
set off, they saw something
dangling in a tree.

"Help!" cried Mouse.

"I'm stuck! The wind blew
me up with my kite! It's so
high, and I'm scared!"

"Hang on, Mouse,"
yelled Alfie. "I'm coming!"

Alfie scrambled
up, up, up,

higher and higher,

and helped Mouse
safely onto a branch.

"Thank you, Alfie," said Mouse.
"You're a hero! But it's such
a long climb down."
"Just hold on to me," said Alfie.
He climbed down to the lowest branch
then wriggled out of his jumper...

"Wheeeeeeeeeeeeeeeeee!"

Alfie and Mouse floated
down to the ground.

"You did it!" shouted Rabbit. "That was very brave, Alfie."

"But my poor jumper – it's ruined!" cried Alfie. "What will your mummy say?" gasped Moley.

"She'll be so sad," thought Alfie as he plodded slowly home in his saggy, baggy jumper.

"I'm sorry," sobbed Alfie when he saw Mummy.
"I've broken my full-of-love jumper!
I didn't mean to."

"I know, darling," smiled Mummy.
"Daddy Rabbit has told me all about your
adventures today! What a kind and helpful
friend you've been ..."

"... I will knit another jumper, full of love, for my **wonderful,** **brave little bear!**"

Tracey Corderoy · Alison Edgson

Just One More!

With a wonderful colour-in storybook!

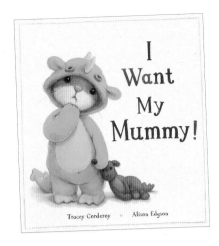

I Want My Mummy!

Tracey Corderoy   Alison Edgson

I Love You More Each Day!

Suzanne Chiew

Tina Macnaughton

Tracey Corderoy · Caroline Pedler

I Can Do It!

for all determined toddlers

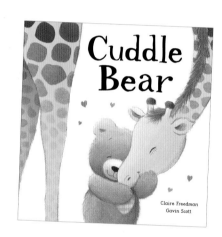

Cuddle Bear

Claire Freedman
Gavin Scott

Jane Chapman
Tim Warnes

Hands off MY HONEY!

More heart-warming stories
from Little Tiger Press

For information regarding any of the above titles
or for our catalogue, please contact us:
Little Tiger Press, 1 The Coda Centre,
189 Munster Road, London SW6 6AW
Tel: 020 7385 6333 • Fax: 020 7385 7333
E-mail: contact@littletiger.co.uk
www.littletiger.co.uk